Viori Publishing

vioripublishing.com

You may contact Ari Meier at
ari@vioripublishing.com

Humping and Releasing: Delicious
Erotic Poetry

Copyright Ari Meier 2014

Published by Viori Publishing

ISBN 978-0-9913432-1-8

Dedications

I dedicate this book to all of the
women and men that embrace
love, the erotic and great sex all in
one wrap.

Love Back Home

I see u
U wanted to
But I wasn't there
I see u
U wanted to
But I wasn't there
Can't get into u
Gotta love back home
She's better than u
Get away from me
Trying to entice me
With your hot violin
Trying to get my guitar all strung up

My Flowers are Blooming Back Home

Leave me alone
I couldn't live with myself
If u had me
No, she wouldn't know
You'd just be a ho
Trying to please me
U can't please a man n love
With yo sticky vagina floor
And big ass shore

Poem dedicated to all of the faithful men.

Y R U Freaking?

Girl what ya doing
Why r u shaking
Yo thang n his face
Your heart is a breaking
U don't need to show it
Your mystical body
If he wants to love u
He'll get to know your heart
Baby- you're so special
U gotta pull it out your inside
U can be strong when you are free
U gotta pull it out your inside
Girl why u freaking
Whimsical r u
Because he wanna do it
Don't let his boy screw it
Stay with your spirit
U only want his love
He won't do right
Kick his ass to the curb
Baby- you're so special
U gotta pull it out your inside
U can b strong when you are free
U gotta pull it out-your inside

Eye'll Come with U

I'll come with u
I'll leave my heart behind
I'll twist it in u
Leave a love denied
Like a jazz flowing motion
And a rock dripping sulphur
We tangle like baby spiders
I get deep n your ocean
I'll come with u
If u'll leave your heart behind
I'll show u my twister
If u don't tell the outside bout the
inside
I know that u'll go
Where I go
U follow the energy
I follow the magic show
Don't scream too loud
When I rope u in my freaky land
Don't bring your heart so close
Cause my twister's insane-it'll bring u
pain
I'll come with u
Leave my heart behind
U show my twister a new thing
My heart's on the verge of pain
I came with u

6

U took my heart away
And beat me about a falling star
day
With our game
Buried deep in the back
Of our pain
I know that u'll go
Where I go
U follow the energy
I follow the magic show
The bright sunshine
Dried my 10 day tears
Wanting to die
When u stole my heart-left me fears
U used my 100 million dollars
to buy u another soul twister
on the riverbank-scream and holler
a frosty heart stomping sista
no more twister show
and 100 million dollar ho
no more twister no
for the heart stealing sista ho

**Dedicated to the dudes who think
they are the playas, but are played.**

Writing Notes from the Edge of Bed

she drove me
i didn't eat for days
she asked me questions of love
only those things that r asked after
the thing
i told her no
she cried, i lied
she held me n her sunshine
everything went lavender
i started to throb past the point
she arched like a cat
screaming n unison with my screams
i told her i was involved
involved?
but why? u told me yes
she was red and turned out

The Pregnant Woman in the Tub

i watched through the cracked door
a pregnant woman bathing
a dripping faucet and splashing tub
singing to me back and forth
this pregnant woman's breasts were
full and they were glistening under
the water
the air smelled of burning candles
and soap
my desires made me smell her
vagina
with each graceful move to clean
herself
i would grab my penis
and hold it tight to keep it from
bursting out of my drawers
it was a nasty scene mixed with pure
glamour girl

Kinda Love Thang

Show me yo underwear
Gotta act like I care
Show me yo underwear
Gotta act like I care
Everything's in speed motion
Making my move
to take a drink of yo ocean
I'll make your body groove
U spend yo time with yo makeup
Wriggling in yo tight skirt
Do U have a pierced tongue
If U do, show me what U do
Baby U kinda young
Not too young for me to do
What U expect, U give it up
Like a money ho
Trading self esteem
for fake love in your door
U spend yo time with yo makeup
Wriggling in yo tight skirt
Now U started drinking juice
Then later U started smoking sticks
to impress yo artificial man
swollen belly & getting sick
his nervous sweat in yo eye
he says U too young

to have one now
but wasn't too young to lay down
U spend yo time with yo makeup
Wriggling in yo tight skirt
Some men are like flies on shit
When they see a tight skirt
Their thinking is below
You're thinking mostly above
U think it's love
Because he gives U a feeling
But he may give others that feeling
He just likes the feeling
U spend yo time with yo makeup
Wriggling in yo tight skirt

**Song dedicated to all the young girls
and women looking for love in all the
wrong places.**

Your Rivers of Explosion Tunes: Respect of the Closed Legs

your beauty fills me with a lust
but i know your rules
i can feel your mind
i beg for your physicality
but i know your rules
your body shape slithers into my ego
dream
still begging for some-- time
and i still know your rules
after our minds meet
our bodies greet
on our night, i realize your head
on our night, i experience your
wholeness
u caress me
u bless me
u become me
i become u
merging rivers n the cosmic forest
explosion
your music is the best- the only
there's no other music- for me
all the other songs sound the same
your love keeps me out of the rain

Underground Smiles: Fuel Midnight Desires

I care about u as my morning
sunshine
Feeling your spirit and mine merging
into one
I know that I've known u throughout
time
There's no other woman for me,
you're the one
Thinking of u:
You make me speak like an animal,
with no language
A cloud and much rain
I'm holding u and my heart's
satisfied
On a heaven level
Giving each other powers to see
Through the flowers and cards
And feel painless hearts and mental
orgasms
When I touch u:
U make me climax deep n my head
Quivering like a strong tree n a windy
forest
Your smiles fuck my old dog into
death

13

Your lips are Indian rainbows,
pecking my native neck
You're my baby, my heart, my
desires
When I breathe, I breathe in your
body, mind and soul
I desire your capture of me
Your love opening, pulling me into
your deepest inside
I desire your emotions, and my
emotions becoming
E Motion
I send out a thought ray to u
I am U
U are me
We be, what we only see
We float on the waves powered by
love, compassion and caring
Controlling their outcomes
COME GROW WITH ME...

Can't Stay Away from Each Other

When I thought of u
Coming into my mind
Then I saw u
So beautiful and divine
-Your spirit so sweet
-Your voice is so meek
And then I touched u
Knowing things wouldn't b the same
Picking cozmyk flowers
Massaging your soul with time
Minutes turn to hours
When we merge our body and mind
-I miss u so much
-When I don't feel your touch
But when I touch u
I can't help myself, u can't help
yourself
Baby, we can't stay away from
each other
And I don't know what to say
We can't stay away from each other
Not a single hour or day
We can't stay away from each other
Still, I don't know what to say
We can't stay away from each other

The hours turn into days
When I lay with u
Looking at our starry sky
Then I see your face
And mine, in the moonlight
-Your love is so strong
-your voice whisper a song
And then I loved u
Stars over our heads, grass as our
bed
Baby, we can't stay away from
each other
And I don't know what to say
We can't stay away from each other
Not a single hour or day
We can't stay away from each other
Still, I don't know what to say
We can't stay away from each other
The hours turn into days

Orgasmic Ocean

Making love to u…is like the feeling
of being in the ocean warm, salty
water, moving in and out, between
my legs
The water caressing my penis,
eventually expressing my juice my
body jerking like an epileptic fit.
Woman u pull out the best n me
Saving it, for your nurturing
Your ocean, so sweet and salty
 I love the rolling of my tongue in
your waves lapping up ur essence,
sharing in your
musical explosion
Caressing your gentle curves, feeling
your face and reading your eyes
Such a woman with a ready smile
and moist heart
Massaging your baby soft back, then
licking your curving back, while
nibbling your juicy melon my penis is
connected to your electricity, it rises
in temperature
U permit it to enter your swirling
ocean…its boiling waves

I'm surfing in your waves and we
brace ourselves to land
A feeling rises from the bottom of
your feet
A feeling rises from my ankles
 We become aware of our landing
Our feelings, so intense, we can't
seem to focus
Heart beats act as big nasty drums
Punctuating our body vibrations...as
we land
Feeling each other as we discover
more of what we want to know

California Girl

I've been watching u
your new hair do's, funky clothes
But, U actually scare me
there's something about U that can
pull me...into orbit
U can encourage me...with a swing
of your back end
To engage into something that will
feel good
something that'll keep us
coming....coming back for more
I've been watching u, though I talk
to u, I don't talk as much as I feel
Because u scare me...in the best
way
When u walk, it's like motion poetry
When u talk, my mind drifts into a
secret imagination
Good imagination, where we
explore our tickle zones
Where I massage your head, u rub
my back
i just wanna nibble your ear, your
neck, your big peach
before u think it's all about the
physical

it's your thinking, the way u smile
u make me blush when I don't want
to
u make me nervous, when I try to be
cool
rather than expose my secret lust
crush, I'd rather keep it hush
u scare me
I secretly paint u with my essence in
my nightly thoughts
I could lose myself, inside u
Addicted is me after tasting u
U don't even know, my thoughts, my
secret passion

What Do U Like?

Who are u?
What do u like?
Do u like candle wax, dripping,
dripping...?
What about honey painted around
your....on your...
U seem like u like being on top,
positioning your part to mine
A perfect fit, a perfect explosion
What if I slide it...in from the
back...the hump
Riding your big apple
Hitting spots that u couldn't do
without the buzzing thing
What do u feel?
Is it just right? Too small, too big
Stabbing u just right?
At this time...it's all about u
U should feel high, to compensate
those times
in the past when u were frustrated,
orgasms that were too shy
Guys that were too sleep and slack
Feel high
I wanna know
What do u like?

I Tried Math, but the Banana Exploded Anyway

Your words slither around me
they're alive calling my name n the
moment
wrapping ourselves into a thousand
screams
u move as a graceful dancer
horizontally trapping me in the box
of "turn out"
your words feed me ego sandwiches
grabbing me, impregnating my soul
love....love....love
my toes, my heels, my stomach,
chest
feeling your energy, in our cocoon
I must think about math now
To hold back, to stop the flow
It's getting harder to hold back
Your juicy melon, communicating
with my throbbing self
Ignoring its eventual explosion
Um...Geometry.....sine...cosine....ta
aangent

Apple Juice

Your eyes they feed me
Notions
Walking past u...I blush
Ideas...feed me
Juicy tilapia and I'm ready
We want each other
I'm scared...of your big apple
And what it means to take a bite
I'll want apple juice...your life
Where were u, when I was one
Now, you're here and your legs
Tell me stories of intellect
And goooood apple juice.
My dreams feature u
in a perfect balance of mind
Soul and body
In the dream, I had u
Underneath...me
We danced n the covers
Then the ring of my clock
Bzzzzzzzz
Wake me from the apple juice...

BrainDiary1: Danger and the Platonic People

MAN
I have a friend, a most delightful one year friend
We hang out in bookstores, cafes and the occasional concert
We're both independently unattached
But lately, I've been feeling....

WOMAN
He's such a cool guy, we hang out
Maybe I'm like "one of the guys" to him
I never have to worry about him hitting on me
In the beginning, I wondered if he might be gay
That notion went up in flames, when....

MAN
Something is itching me, deep in my mind

24

About this woman, she wore
something the other day
That caught my manhood
This anxious feeling rose to the
surface

WOMAN
He gave me his major eyes
After seeing me in my...fitting mini
and heels
I felt funny, and I had a heavy inside
smile
I wonder what he...

MAN
People already think that we're
bound together
It's how close we stand in the public
space
Sometimes I catch her eyes, looking
down
Anxious energy, center on my piece
Sizing her at the rear, the front, I feel
light

WOMAN
Think I'll position myself, for a show
I feel a little anxious, thinking about
his energy

Feelings can destroy a beautiful
thing
If it's so good I'll want more
Conflict of the highest

MAN
She's serving me her specialty, my
friend
Possibilities of the evening creep into
a hungry mind
She's got ambiance, I've got nerves,
that won't calm
She's wearing another mini, with legs
screaming out for me to caress
Hmmm....

WOMAN
My ass feels like it's on fire, when I
walk past him
Will he make a move? I smile with
thoughts of him
Spreading me out, right now, with
the carpet as our bed
Anxiousness is my close friend now
As I sit close...

MAN
Horny-ness, replaces hunger as my
friend

While gazing into her most beautiful
eyes
I whisper: I want u
She smiles, now anxiety goes away
with a knowing...

WOMAN
He plants a kiss near the back of my
neck
I feel a rush from my toes, up my
back
He's dangerous and I feel like I want
danger
Wetness is what I feel...

MAN
I catch her luscious lips, and our
tongues dance like nasty teens
I nibble every part of her
Parts that she was unaware had
those kinds of feelings

MAN AND WOMAN
We did things that the dark only
knows
We felt things that our bodies and
minds, can't seem to compare with
our past
We were reborn that night

We cried and passed out
Our experience is the secret and the
connection to our continued good
friendship....

BrainDiary2: The Continuation of the Connection

MAN
I'm in the bed, thinking
Looking at the ceiling
I see her, dancing gracefully
My friend, but now, she's MY FRIEND
Can't get her out of my mind
Our connection…is getting stronger

WOMAN
I wonder what he's doing….thinking
Can't get him out of my…head
When we merge, the memory can't escape me
My body was aching for him…I didn't know

MAN
Passing her desk, my heart races, memories of our nights make me stop
I can't help myself, looking into her eyes, our knowing secret
Ideas are popping up…at the job

Where can I take her? I'm so feeling
to be inside of softness

WOMAN
Seeing him, is different...after he
touched me
I wanna rub him as he walks past my
desk
my thinking makes me like a juicy
mango
there must be a place....
A special spot, cuddle spot

MAN AND WOMAN
We did the unthinkable...after
finding a barren, dark room
The room was the center of our silent
scream cinema
It felt good and felt scary....her on
me/ him on me, in the twirling chair
Doing it like it's the last time ever
The sound of our muffled breaths
and slippery bodies, scream out of
the stillness
Then, there's release....

BrainDiary3: Conflict Brewing a New Coffee Hell

MAN AND WOMAN
We're flowing, still knowing
Our times in secret rooms
It keeps getting better, our loving

WOMAN
This other guy's starting to bother me
His questions dealing with intimacy
Whether my friend and I have gone there
His girlfriend works with us
Knowing nothing of his affections for me
But he had his chance....right?

MAN
My love for my friend explodes red
Sometimes, I feel that something's missing
Like she's not telling me something
There's another energy around her
I long for more mango, juicy mango

31

WOMAN
Though there's nothing going on
with us....anymore
He's asking about my friend
Wanting to know what part of me
have I shared
None of your business-you girlfriend
wracked wreck
He's....

ANOTHER MAN
Why and what do u see in this "man
thing"
U know what I feel, my feelings I
won't conceal
Giving this strange man your time
and fruit
Remember our times, the parking
garage, u releasing 3 times
I miss u, I want u
I dream u and our passion
I hear u and your screams
Let's do our thing
Forget his strangeness, he's a punk

Brain Diary4: Comeback of the Twista and the Eventual Elimination

OTHER MAN:
Gotta have more of u, a little some
at least
While making love to my girl, on a
hot moon night
I was thinking of u, our times, and
twists.
Gotta have u, be in u....

WOMAN:
Your chance was in your lap, a few
seasons back
But remember, your girl that u
wanted to respect
The one with the arrow at your heart
I don't remember when u crossed
my mind....

OTHER MAN:
Your legs, I must kiss...

WOMAN:
Your twista, I don't miss...

But you did hit it right, in the
basement, while your girl slept
upstairs

OTHER MAN
But you turned me out, in the
basement, while my girl slept
upstairs.

WOMAN:
I don't feel....

OTHER MAN:
Like dancing? It's a mind thang.
What u feel is the emptiness after me
The non-connection to
that....spaceman
I long to massage your wholeness,
face, thighs, booty
And U miss my tongue, slithering
around and in your cupcake....

WOMAN:
Your tongue WAS the orgasm mafia
hit squad
Touching parts of my cupcake, parts
not known
But your chance was in your lap,
until your choice

Your choice, screamed the end of
our time

Brain Diary5: The Future of Love, Massages and a Room on the 6th Floor

MAN:
What's on your mind, it's heavy with fear
I know that I've been busy with the sounds and art pieces
But, ur still living in my brain
My body's n pain from ur absence

WOMAN:
Well, it's like....he....

MAN:
He?

WOMAN:
Well, my old work boyfriend, is sniffing me
Telling me things, about this about that
My heart's dim to his bull-shit-ology
He just wants some....

MAN:
Pussycat...tales don't please me
Ur hiding a deeper energy
within...let's talk
I'm sorry for my time being short with
u
If I could only hold u...some more
If only I could kiss ur beautiful,
luscious lips, some more
Remember how we could gaze into
each other's eyes and soul
So intensely, that we could come

WOMAN:
I miss u, your massages, your
warmness, your...tongue, your penis
I miss your words, our candle incense
sauna baths
Our bathtub adventure-sexing
The way u ate fruit down there and
your nose massaging me...to orgasm

MAN:
All this talk, uhhmmm, got me in a
position
Like meet me on floor 6, lunchtime,
personal services room
One at a time, glad that u wore your
skirt today, uhhmmm

Haven't had u in, a few days, can't
stay away from u

WOMAN:
I'll take u ALL in, my lips sealing u in
Taking u almost to the point
Then spreading my legs, skirt up high
I'll bring u into my fat, wet juiciness

WOMAN AND MAN:
In our friction town, we are the
magnets
Merging into each other, we wanted
to make love
In our short time, we must fuck
And fucking, we are
In this moment, I felt like I completely
lost my mind
But it's good, it can't get any better
than this....
I feel the pressure building within
From my toes, rising
My lips form a frown, like I'm crying
And.... I'm saying..... ohhhhh shitttttttt

Potentials of Something Deeper Happening from Having Rose Petals Forming a Trail at the 6pm Door

When she gets home, the moment is a secret
What looks like a piece of paper on the floor, is a rose petal
Then 2, then 3 and so on....making a trail of excited mind eroticas
When she gets to the bedroom door, a note is found hanging on it
This note gives explicit directions on her next move.
She's to remove her top and socks.
Inside the bedroom, another note comes whispering at her from the dresser top
It directs her to remove her bra and skirt
(Her inside is pounding with the enthusiasm of a young girl sneaking out of her window)
She hears music, a deep slow pounding music

The rose petal trail leads her towards
the bathroom
There's a note on the closed door...it
says "covered skin is forbidden past
this point"
She has aroma
Removing her last piece of clothing
and opening the bathroom door,
She sees that the rose petals lead to
the bathtub...which is filled with
more petals
and her serious man
She has more aroma...sliding into the
warm bubbly water
They get tender and feel each other
She explores every inch of him and
they play lips and tongues
Scooping up his juicy love, water
soaked floor
She has aroma, he straightens out all
the way
He opens her, placing his nose down
to her love taking in deep cocaine
breaths...she gives
more aroma
Then he French kisses her love, while
he's straight to the sky
She screams and creams

Her love sauce is parted with a
whisper
They lock eyes
He's immersed in her cream of treat
They tangle on and on in the wet
living bed
Drenched from their merged session
(Rim shots are her thing)
Her mind and body become 1
His mind and body become 1
The 1+1 becomes 1
 (She opens her mouth, closing her
eyes tightly)
Then came the waters, surrounding
him
He's outta his mind, he's outta his
mind, he's outta his mind!

SexWorkParade

I knew she would do it. I saw it in her eye when I was on the computer too long Friday night. It's just like her to do it and I shouldn't be the least surprised. After making more corrections on my book and reading forums, blogs, emails, social media and reading more emails, I finally rolled into bed about 4 am. Everything seemed innocent enough and quiet. But I knew that she'd make a move and she'd make that move when I mostly expected it.

Sure enough my sleep was broken by fingers, a hand. This hand rubbed my leg, then on the bottom of my stomach. I turned my head to look at the clock, 5:30. I thought, maybe she doesn't want to do it, that maybe it's a middle of the sleep hand outta control.

Her hand reached my stiffening rod, caressing it with a strong sexual urge caress. I knew that I wouldn't be going back to my slumber right away. I'm not complaining about my stiff rod and the fact that it's stiff most of the time, but like most men say about their rods, it's stiff without any provocation early in the morning.

Her molesting hand rubbed my hard stick as the sleepiness slowly left my body in anticipation of the upcoming horizontal hump dance. I couldn't help but to remember how often we've been having sex lately and how this started happening.

I was soon lying on my back and she crouched over me, while pulling her panties off. With the sound of the panties coming, my penis' hardness was intensified. She started grinding on my hardness and I got more aroused with feeling her juices on me.

Five thirty seven. This middle of the night man molester slowly slid her hot juicy stuff over my rod, slowly rising and falling on it like a nasty sunset and sunrise. She threw her back into the humping, and it was hard. I felt good, especially as I was too sleepy to do a lot, except maybe move a little while on my back. She kept at it for a few minutes, and then stopped abruptly, instructing me not to move.

She wasn't ready to come yet and I started thinking about if she was going to work in a few hours and I wanted us to check out the festival around noonish. I must get at least six hours of sleep.

She started humping again and with each thrust, I would feel the goodness of her juices running down the sides of my rod and onto my crotch area. She humped harder and started looking at the wall, while breathing heavily.

She let out a moan as she came strongly and spilling more juice onto my member. I'm thinking at this moment that I'll get my nut and we can both roll over and finish our sleep. Oh no, not "Miss I wanna come some more before we're done". She rolled my sleep heavy body over onto her, while positioning me between her moist thighs. I somehow summoned up some energy to throw a little more of my back, (just a little) into our horizontal hump dance.

I thrusted deep into her, then she stopped me. Again, she wanted to build up the orgasm strength. We started humping harder, harder, then she let out a moan as she tensed her body to let the climax roll through her like a wave, then I came hard, while pulling out right before I shot my load. As I was coming, I grinded on her lips, while going through my orgasmic jerks, she squeezed out the remaining load.

I awakened to not less than two good sleep in the morning no-no's: a screaming overhead light and an "I'm going to work and can you drop me off voice." I'm thinking that I'll drop her off at the train station, which would get me back in my bed in less than ten minutes. She instead, wanted me to drop her off at the job, which is about a fourteen minute roundtrip. It seemed to take her forever to decide on what to wear and she intermittedly harassed me about leaving soon and putting on my clothes.

Putting on my clothes was the easiest part and even getting out of bed was not so bad. It was the harsh greeting from the early morning sun and heat that made me feel like I was being attacked. As we drove down the street, we noticed crowds of people lining the streets as if either a parade just happened or was about to happen.

I'm a parade person and got curious and awakened more. Dragon*con! Dragon*con's in town and this was the annual parade. My excitement caused me to blurt out, "I'm checking this parade out". But I didn't want to go to the parade wearing my pajama-like shorts. My excitement grew as I saw groups of

Star Wars characters marching on the sidewalks, while sporadic cheers rang from walking spectators. I rushed home, got online and googled "Dragon con" while hoping that I hadn't missed the parade or that it wouldn't start right away. My parade freak ass, yelled when I saw that the parade wouldn't start until ten and it was about nine twenty. I quickly showered, put on clothes and picked my hair.

I cranked up my iPod, grabbed my bag, and walked out the door heading to the subway. I mused for a few minutes on the popularity of the "man-bags" or carrier bags. Amazed at how ahead of the current trends my non fashionista ass has been.

But then I'm a bag collector, like how women like collecting their pocketbook and purses, my collecting freakdom is backpacks and backpack-like bags. I must have had ten bags at one time, until nostalgia was replaced with being more practical. Eight minutes and three April March songs later, I'm descending down into the hot subway station, where I see Alabama and Clemson fans and Dragon*con-like people standing, waiting on the metal human carrying snake.

After a six minute ride, listening to the out of towners muse about the upcoming game and looking nervously in my direction, I took the elevator up to the street (because I don't like riding the long escalator at this station, it makes me get vertigo half way up) and saw many people lined up on both sides of the street.

I was amazed at the number of people that showed up for the parade and I made a mental note comparing the amount of people here with the number of people at other parades. It seemed to have similar numbers of people between the Dragon*con parade and the Christmas parade. The parade reached my section about five minutes later and I started snapping pictures from my phone. The Dragon*con parade is always a freaky affair and the beautiful thing about it is there are no corporation bought floats with their propaganda in the parade or politicians blasting you with their bullshit about voting for them, the closest thing that was in the parade to that type of craziness, was the occasional politician spoof riding through.

I experienced the child like excitement of seeing the Justice League Super heroes, two Santa Clauses, faeries, Star Wars characters, Battlestar Galactica characters, strange and unknown aliens and horror figures.

The parade lasted for nearly an hour and afterwards my starving stomach called for a trip across the street to McDonalds. After waiting in line for about 40 minutes, I finally got up to the counter. I listened to this woman behind me complain about "how slow the workers are moving" to that

McDonald's seemingly lack of planning in handling this anticipated large crowd. She complained and her anger grew with each second and I wanted so much to tell her to shut the fuck up and either deal with the service or get the fuck on.

Her boyfriend or husband provided the long needed balance of her continual bitching session by interjecting about the costliness of the McDonalds hiring more workers for high traffic occasions when the current staffing levels are sufficient maybe 90 percent of the time.

I ordered a chicken sandwich meal and decided at the last minute to get one apple pie. The young and flirtatious cashier tried selling me on getting two of the pies as they were on sale for 2 for one dollar. She told me that one pie would cost more than two and I got a little pissed as I couldn't see the logic. I felt as if McDonalds was trying to get my ass fat with a deal like that as I couldn't see the logic of them selling two pies for cheaper than one pie and making money off of the deal. "Of course they must be trying to stress out my pancreas with the two pies", screamed my paranoid mind.

By this time getting only four hours sleep was getting the best of my body and it didn't help to know that I wouldn't go home and go to sleep because I wanted to be at the festival around 12ish.

I texted my girlfriend to tell her that I was across the street from her job and that we'll be riding the train home together and when I walked out on the sidewalk, I looked ahead and saw a familiar face. It was my coworker from my last serious job.

Though I didn't know her well, as she worked on a floor that I rarely visited, she gave me an "I know you" hug and we exchanged quick words. She asked me about where I was with my music and life and I asked her about her current job. She's a website content creator and maintainer at one of the local colleges, but she shied away from being called a web master (or webmistress).

I pulled out my book proof and listened to her as she complimented my effort and she seemed genuinely impressed. She wanted to keep in touch with me and told me that she'd send me an email with her blog addresses.

I wanted to keep in touch with her because of her being a web geek. We said bye to each other and I crossed the street. My girl burst forth through the office building's front door after about five minutes of waiting and we descended into the subway station by way of the piss smelling elevator.

Climbing Trees

What wind blows the sex?
A wind red and yellow
A stiffness swinging in the canvas of
my underwear
What wind blows the sex?
A wind that captures a big brown
bad booty
Humping under me, punctuated by
my stiffness
That's swinging in the tapestry of her
thang

I Dream the Dream

I had a dream about you
About what we could do
You have a tingle down there
And me pulling your hair
Girl you are so beautiful
As a purple rose
I have a feeling down there
I wanna pull your hair
When I need the sunshine
Hold your hand and understand
We give each other light
My special woman
I dream the dream
Of minds serene
You'll ask me why
I change the scene
I will hold you tight
In this bottom wet night
It makes much sense to me
We give each other light
Your rhythms' so sweet
No one can compete
I yelled, you screamed
You rained down on the nasty scene
You shook and quaked
You scratched my neck
I curled my toes

54

Sugar bang sugar
I dream the dream
Of minds serene
You'll ask me why
I change the scene

The Thing

I found her to be sexually stimulating
She would indulge in long periods of
hand touching, caressing both my
inner and outer worlds.
She tried to resist my appeal which
would only draw her closer to me in
many ways.
But did she jump?
Jumped all over it!
Over what?
Over it.
You mean the thing?
Yes, it. The thing.
Did she like it?
She says she did.
Was that it?

The Fream (fuck-dream) I had when I was Young

She beamed at my face
Looking only for something
I asked her for that thing
She told me the place
Scruffy tights with tired lips
Quiver butt and floppy breasts
Pass it to her
Future of rocking hips
We settle as animals of the farm
This mechanized fuck tank
She flies open with screaming juices
Wondering if she's all harm
Tantalizing rhythms and tickle toes
Rocking as two babies with sense
She took my mind to other shores
 And left my body with no defense
I couldn't love her because of the money
Others would have the money
Getting all my 15 minute honey
I looked at this face
Looking up at me
What could I do?
We've screamed-too late!

Ring, ring, ringing-waking me from
this thing
This evil dripping thing
Soaking me and almost
embarrassing me
She only allow 15, but gave me 30
Afterwards we created pyramids in
our dreams

www.ingramcontent.com/pod-product-compliance
Lightning Source LLC
Chambersburg PA
CBHW020319150626
46552CB00022B/3014